P9-CRZ-053

Night in the Barn

Faye Gibbons ILLUSTRATED BY Erick Ingraham

MORROW JUNIOR BOOKS NEW YORK

Varnished watercolors were used for the full-color illustrations.
The text type is 16.5-point Amerigo Medium.

Inquiries should be addressed to William Morrow and Company, Inc., 1350 Avenue of the Americas, New York, NY 10019.
Printed in the United States of America.
1 2 3 4 5 6 7 8 9 10

Library of Congress Cataloging-in-Publication Data
Gibbons, Faye. Night in the barn/Faye Gibbons; illustrated by Erick Ingraham. p. cm.
Summary: Four boys set out to prove they are not afraid to spend the night in the big, cold, dark barn.
ISBN 0-688-13326-6 (trade)—ISBN 0-688-13327-4 (library)
[1. Barns—Fiction. 2. Night—Fiction. 3. Fear of the dark—Fiction.] I. Ingraham, Erick, ill.
II. Title. PZ7.G33913Ni 1995 [E]—dc20 94-43776 CIP AC

For Andrea Curley—
Best of editors, best of friends.

—F.G.

It was darker than dark that cold fall night. The stars hid behind windswept clouds, and the moon was a here-again, gone-again eye.

"Bet you're afraid," said my big brother, Willie, to me and our city cousins, Julius and Dan. "Bet you're afraid to spend the night in the barn."

"Not me," said Dan.

"Not me," said Julius.

"M-m-me neither," I said.

So we gathered up sleeping bags, snacks, and coats and headed for the back door. Our dog, Amos, was waiting there, his tail *pat-pat-patting* a question.

"No," Willie told him, grabbing the flashlight. "You can't go. You'll eat our food and drool on our sleeping bags."

I gave Amos a good-night hug, then walked out to the porch and down the stairs. My breath was a fog in the frosty air.

Ooooooo moaned the wind through the orchard trees.

Rustle, rustle went something in the garden hedge.

"Just a possum, Mike," Willie said to me, and started to run.
"Yeah," I agreed, but I hurried to catch up with him.

We all slid to a stop at the big barn door, where the shadows were deep and the wind was cold.

"Wanna go back?" Willie said.

"Not me," said Dan.

"Not me," said Julius.

Ooooooo moaned the wind.

"So, you ready?" Willie asked. I could feel him looking right at me.

"S-sure," I said.

The barn door creaked when Willie lifted the latch. It groaned when I pulled it back. It banged when the wind slammed it against the wall.

I leaned into the barn to show how brave I was. It was darker than dark in there, though moonlight oozed through cracks and gaps all around.

I stepped inside and froze. In a far corner, two glowing eyes looked straight at me.

"Me-e-*ow*!" squalled a neighbor's cat as it shot between my legs and out into the night.

Ghosts and monsters lurked on every side, ready to lunge and pounce.

Then Willie clicked on the flashlight. In the dancing circle of light the ghosts and monsters turned into boxes of canning jars, stacks of lumber, and pieces of furniture.

We tiptoed through the barn, inching across the uneven floor. I swung around when something touched my ear—and slapped at a dangling spiderweb.

We crept up the sloping steps to the loft, counting every stair: "One, two, three, four, five, six . . ."

Ooooooo moaned the wind through the hay in the loft.

"Sure is big up here," said Julius.

"Sure is cold," said Dan.

"Sure is dark," I said.

We spread our sleeping bags side by side, next to a bale of hay, and crawled in with all our clothes on. We told scary stories, ate Cheesy Crispies, and made shadow figures on the wall until the flashlight began to dim.

"Guess it's time for lights out," Willie said, clicking off the flashlight and laying it on the floor.

"That's okay with me," I said, but the barn turned dark again, and night sounds crept in close.

Who-oo-oo-oo, who-oo-oo-oo came a call from the far side of the pasture.

Julius turned on the flashlight.

"Shut that off," said Willie. "It's just an owl."

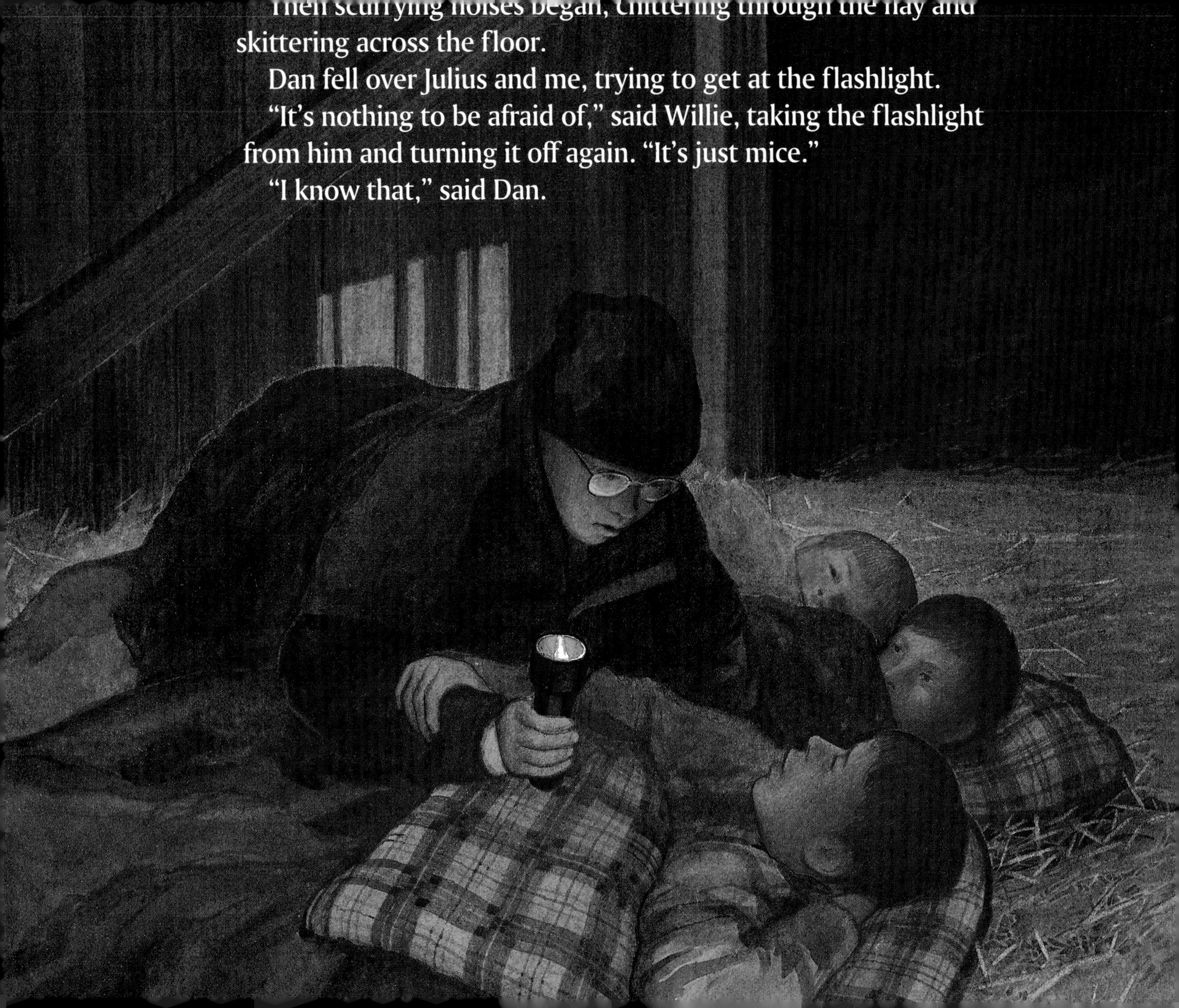

Then scurrying noises began, chittering through the hay and skittering across the floor.

Dan fell over Julius and me, trying to get at the flashlight.

"It's nothing to be afraid of," said Willie, taking the flashlight from him and turning it off again. "It's just mice."

"I know that," said Dan.

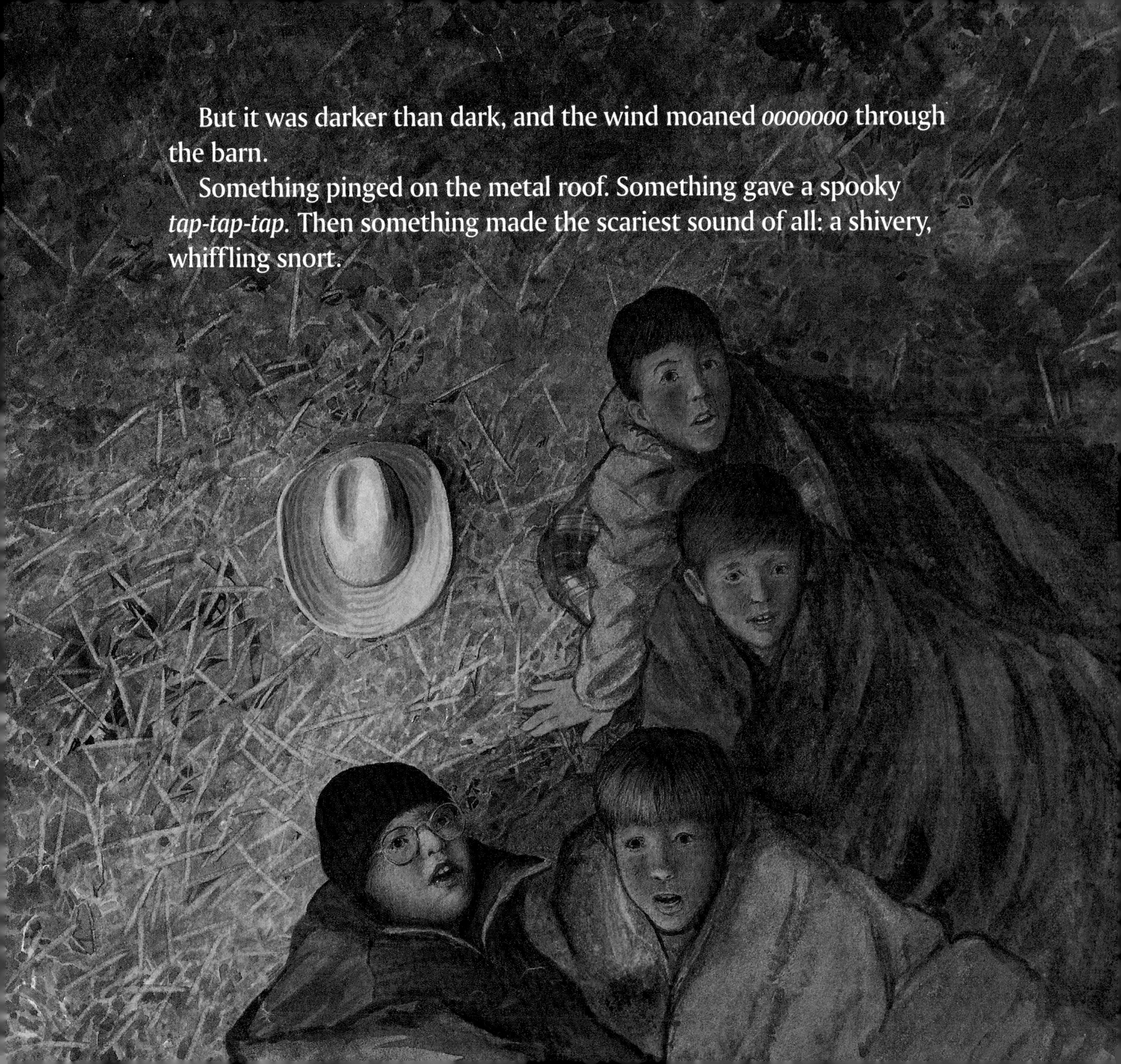

But it was darker than dark, and the wind moaned *ooooooo* through the barn.

Something pinged on the metal roof. Something gave a spooky *tap-tap-tap*. Then something made the scariest sound of all: a shivery, whiffling snort.

We all dived for the flashlight. Somebody got it and somebody dropped it.

"Oh, no," I whispered as the flashlight *clunk-clunk-clunked* down the steps and hit the floor below.

Willie grabbed my arm. "Mike, did you leave the barn door open?" he whispered.

"Me?" I said.

But there was no time to argue. Something was shuffling across the floor below.

Something was snuffling up the steps. Something was coming straight for us in the loft.

I saw a shadowy shape just as it leaped at Willie and Dan and Julius and me.

We all screamed together.

Then something dropped a flashlight on my nose and said, *"Ruff!"*
"Amos!" I cried, turning my face away from our dog's wet tongue. "Down, boy! Down!"

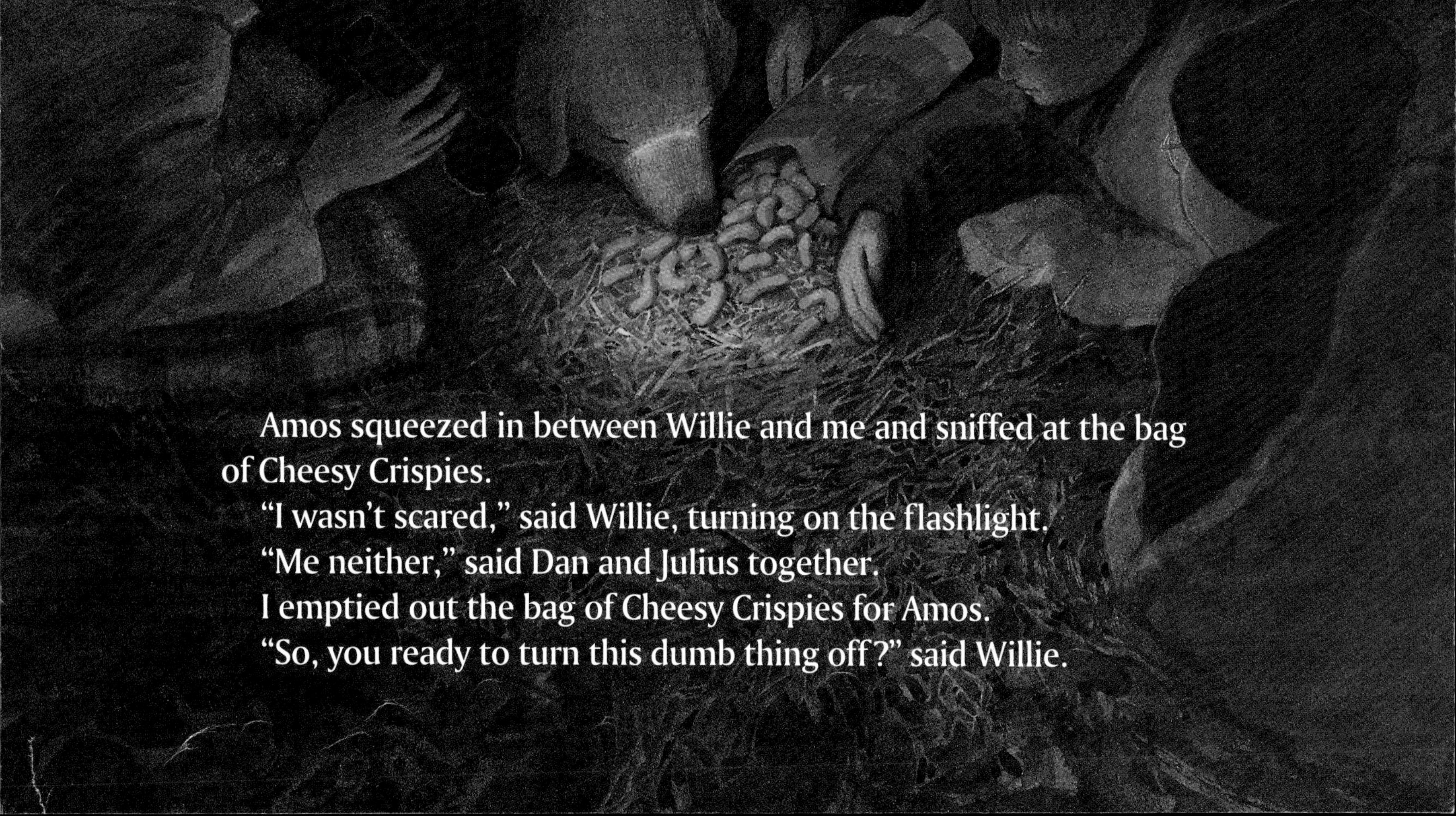

Amos squeezed in between Willie and me and sniffed at the bag of Cheesy Crispies.

"I wasn't scared," said Willie, turning on the flashlight.

"Me neither," said Dan and Julius together.

I emptied out the bag of Cheesy Crispies for Amos.

"So, you ready to turn this dumb thing off?" said Willie.

"Sure," I said, curling up next to Amos.
In the darkness, I heard Willie curl up to him too.